187219

PowerKids Readers:

# The Bilingual Library of the United States of America™

Bilingual Edition
English/Spanish
Edición bilingüe

# IDAHO

**VANESSA BROWN**

TRADUCCIÓN AL ESPAÑOL: MARÍA CRISTINA BRUSCA

The Rosen Publishing Group's
PowerKids Press™ & **Editorial Buenas Letras**™
New York

Published in 2005 by The Rosen Publishing Group, Inc.
29 East 21st Street, New York, NY 10010

First Edition

Photo Credits: Cover, p. 30 ("It Is Forever") © Tom Algire/SuperStock Inc.; p. 5 © Joe Sohm/The Image Works; p. 7 © 2002 Geoatlas; pp. 9, 25, 30 (Capital, The Gem State) © Kevin R. Morris/Corbis; p. 11 © Raymond Gehman/Corbis; pp. 13, 15, 17, 31 (Sacajawea, Chief Joseph, Church, Explorers) © Bettmann/Corbis; pp. 19 (Rafting), 31 (To Raft) © Ariel Skelley/Corbis; p. 21 © Michael S. Yamashita/Corbis; p. 23 © Leon Pantenburg/Index Stock Imagery, Inc.; pp. 26, 30 (Syringa) © Tania Midgley/Corbis; p. 30 (Mountain Bluebird) © D. Robert and Lorri Franz/Corbis; p. 30 (Western White Pine) © Galen Rowell/Corbis; pp. 30 (Star Garnet), 31 (Gemstone) © Ludovic Maisant/Corbis; p. 31 (Borglum) © Corbis; p. 31 (Simplot) © AP/Wide World Photos; p. 31 (Street) © Duomo/Corbis.

Library of Congress Cataloging-in-Publication Data

Brown, Vanessa, 1963–
Idaho / Vanessa Brown ; traducción al español, María Cristina Brusca. —1st ed.
p. cm. — (The bilingual library of the United States of America) Includes bibliographical references (p. ) and index.
ISBN 1-4042-3077-7 (library binding)
1. Idaho–Juvenile literature. I. Title. II. Series.
F746.3.B76 2005
979.6–dc22

2005006098

Manufactured in the United States of America

Due to the changing nature of Internet links, Editorial Buenas Letras has developed an online list of Web sites related to the subject of this book. This site is updated regularly. Please use this link to access the list:

http://www.buenasletraslinks.com/ls/idaho

# Contents

# Contenido

## Welcome to Idaho

These are the flag and the seal of the state of Idaho. The seal has the state motto *Esto perpetua*. This means "It is forever."

---

## Bienvenidos a Idaho

Estos son la bandera y el escudo de Idaho. En el escudo está escrito el lema del estado, *Esto perpetua*, que quiere decir, "Es eterno".

# The Idaho Flag and the State Seal

Bandera y escudo de Idaho

## Idaho Geography

Idaho borders the states of Oregon, Washington, Montana, Wyoming, Utah, and Nevada. In the north, Idaho borders the country of Canada.

---

## Geografía de Idaho

Idaho linda con los estados de Oregón, Washington, Utah y Nevada. En el norte, Idaho comparte una frontera con otro país, Canadá.

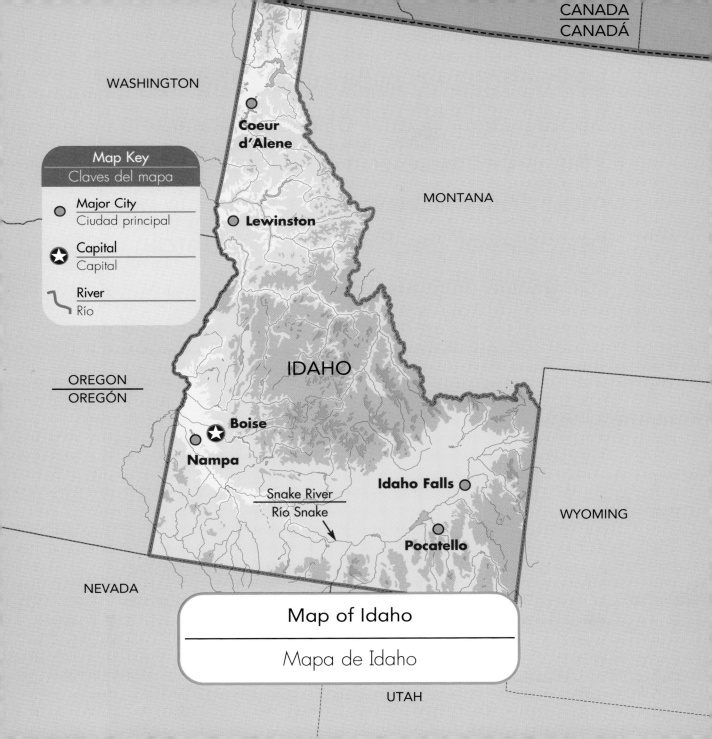

CANADA
CANADÁ

WASHINGTON

Coeur d'Alene

## Map Key
### Claves del mapa

- ○ Major City
  Ciudad principal
- ★ Capital
  Capital
- ～ River
  Río

MONTANA

○ Lewinston

OREGON
OREGÓN

IDAHO

★ Boise
○ Nampa

Idaho Falls ○

WYOMING

Snake River
Río Snake

○ Pocatello

NEVADA

## Map of Idaho

## Mapa de Idaho

UTAH

Idaho has two nicknames, the "Gem State" and "Gem of the Mountains." This is because some of Idaho's mountains have gemstones. It is also because of the beautiful mountain ranges in the state.

---

Idaho tiene dos sobrenombres, el Estado Gema y la Gema de las Montañas. Se le llama así porque en algunas de las montañas de Idaho hay piedras preciosas. Y también porque el estado tiene hermosas cadenas de montañas.

Clearwater Mountains in the Salmon Valley, Idaho

Montañas Clearwater en el valle Salmon, en Idaho

Idaho has many rivers. The longest is the Snake River. This river is an important natural resource for the state. It supplies water to ranchers and farmers.

---

En Idaho hay muchos ríos. El más largo es el río Snake. Este río es una ayuda natural importante para el estado. El río provee de agua a los rancheros y a los agricultores.

**The Snake River**

---

El río Snake

## Idaho History

In 1805, Meriwether Lewis and William Clark became the first white explorers to enter Idaho. They were looking for a trail to the Pacific Ocean.

---

## Historia de Idaho

Meriwether Lewis y William Clark fueron los primeros exploradores blancos en llegar a Idaho, en 1805. Estaban buscando una ruta para llegar al océano Pacífico.

**Lewis and Clark Trip**

El viaje de Lewis y Clark

Sacagawea was a Shoshone Indian. She helped Lewis and Clark on their trip. Sacagawea knew the land and spoke the language of Native American groups.

---

Sacagawea fue una indígena de la tribu Shoshone. Sacagawea ayudó a Lewis y Clark durante su viaje. Sacagawea conocía la región y hablaba el idioma de los nativos americanos.

Sacagawea Guiding Lewis and Clark

Sacagawea guiando a Lewis y Clark

In 1806, E. D. Pierce found gold on Orofino Creek, Idaho. The discovery of gold brought many settlers to the state. Cities in Idaho grew very fast after the discovery of gold.

---

En 1806, E. D. Pierce encontró oro en Orofino Creek, Idaho. El descubrimiento del oro atrajo a muchos pobladores al estado. Después del descubrimiento del oro las ciudades de Idaho crecieron rápidamente.

## Horses and Wagons Arrive in Idaho

Caballos y carretas llegan a Idaho

## Living in Idaho

Idaho's wild nature attracts many visitors. People looking for adventure hike and practice winter sports in the mountains. People also raft and fish in Idaho's rivers.

---

## La vida en Idaho

La naturaleza de Idaho atrae a muchos visitantes. La gente en busca de aventuras sale de excursión y practica deportes invernales en las montañas. La gente también pesca y navega en balsa en los ríos de Idaho.

Idaho grows more potatoes than any other state does. One-third of all the potatoes in the United States come from Idaho.

---

En Idaho se cultivan más papas que en cualquier otro estado. Una tercera parte de todas las papas de los Estados Unidos proviene de Idaho.

Storehouse Full of Potatoes

Depósito lleno de papas

Idaho's population is growing fast. Latinos, or people from Spanish-speaking countries, are the fastest-growing group in the state. Many Latinos come to Idaho to work on the fields and in other jobs.

---

La población de Idaho está creciendo con rapidez. Los latinos, o personas que vienen de países donde se habla español, son el grupo que crece más rápidamente en el estado. Muchos latinos vienen a Idaho a trabajar en los cultivos y en otras tareas.

Latino Workers Harvesting Onions

Trabajadores latinos cosechando cebollas

Boise, Pocatello, Idaho Falls, and Nampa are important cities in Idaho. Boise is the state's most populated city. It is also the capital of the state.

---

Boise, Pocatello, Idaho Falls y Nampa son ciudades importantes de Idaho. Boise es la ciudad más populosa del estado. Es también la capital del estado.

State Capitol Building in Boise, Idaho

Capitolio del estado en Boise, Idaho

# Activity:
## Let's Draw Idaho's State Flower

The Syringa became Idaho's State Flower in 1931.

---

# Actividad:
## Dibujemos la flor del estado de Idaho

La jeringuilla ha sido la flor del estado de Idaho desde 1931.

**1**

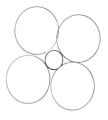

Start by drawing a circle for the center of the flower.

Comienza por dibujar un círculo, en el lugar del centro de la flor.

**2**

Add four circles around the center. Try not to let them overlap.

Agrega cuatro círculos alrededor del centro. Trata de que no se encimen.

**3**

Draw the shape of the petals in the circles as shown.

Dibuja la forma de los pétalos adentro de los círculos, como en el ejemplo.

**4**

Connect the circles.

Conecta los círculos.

**5**

Add pointed leaves. Then erase extra lines from the petals.

Añade hojas en forma de triángulos. Luego, borra de los pétalos las líneas innecesarias.

**6**

Add shading and detail to your flower.

Agrega sombras y detalles a tu flor.

# Timeline

# Cronología

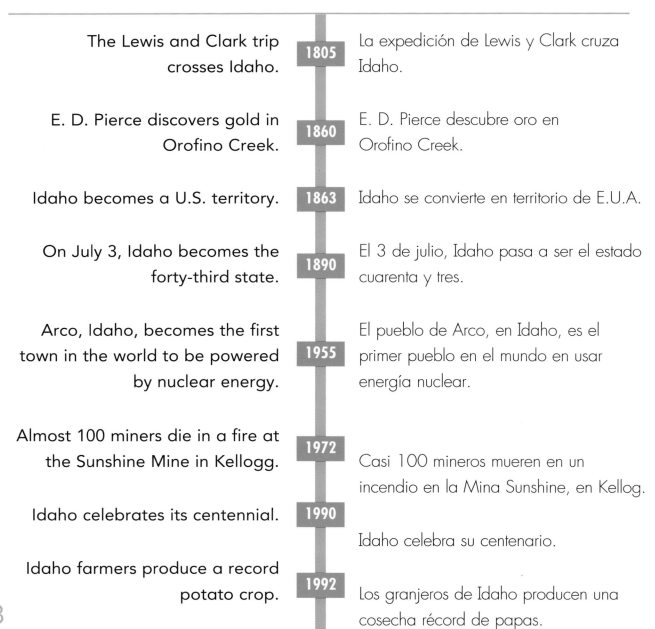

**1805** The Lewis and Clark trip crosses Idaho.

La expedición de Lewis y Clark cruza Idaho.

**1860** E. D. Pierce discovers gold in Orofino Creek.

E. D. Pierce descubre oro en Orofino Creek.

**1863** Idaho becomes a U.S. territory.

Idaho se convierte en territorio de E.U.A.

**1890** On July 3, Idaho becomes the forty-third state.

El 3 de julio, Idaho pasa a ser el estado cuarenta y tres.

**1955** Arco, Idaho, becomes the first town in the world to be powered by nuclear energy.

El pueblo de Arco, en Idaho, es el primer pueblo en el mundo en usar energía nuclear.

**1972** Almost 100 miners die in a fire at the Sunshine Mine in Kellogg.

Casi 100 mineros mueren en un incendio en la Mina Sunshine, en Kellog.

**1990** Idaho celebrates its centennial.

Idaho celebra su centenario.

**1992** Idaho farmers produce a record potato crop.

Los granjeros de Idaho producen una cosecha récord de papas.

| Idaho Events | Eventos en Idaho |
| --- | --- |
| **January**<br>Sun Valley Winter Carnival | Enero<br>Carnaval de invierno de Sun Valley |
| **February**<br>Lionel Hampton Jazz Festival<br>in Moscow | Febrero<br>Festival de jazz Lionel Hampton,<br>en Moscow |
| **March**<br>Harriman Cup in Sun Valley | Marzo<br>Copa Harriman, en Sun Valley |
| **May**<br>Cinco de Mayo in Caldwell<br>Mat Alyma Pow Wow and<br>Root Feast in Kamiah | Mayo<br>Cinco de Mayo, en Caldwell<br>Pow Wow Mat Alyma y Fiesta de las<br>raíces, en Kamiah |
| **June**<br>Magic Valley Dairy Days in Wendell | Junio<br>Días de los lácteos de Magic Valley, en<br>Wendell |
| **July**<br>Shoshone Sun Dances at<br>Fort Hall Reservations | Julio<br>Danzas Shoshone al sol en la reservación<br>Fort Hall |
| **October**<br>Trailing of the Sheep Festival<br>in Ketchum | Octubre<br>Festival de las ovejas, en Ketchum |
| **November**<br>Festival of Trees in Coeur d'Alene<br>Winter Spirit Festival of Lights<br>in Lewinston | Noviembre<br>Festival de los árboles, en Coeur d'Alene<br>Festival de las luces del Espíritu del<br>Invierno, en Lewinston |

# Idaho Facts/Datos sobre Idaho

<u>Population</u>
1.2 million

<u>Población</u>
1.2 millones

<u>Capital</u>
Boise

<u>Capital</u>
Boise

<u>State Motto</u>
*Esto perpetua*
"It is forever"

<u>Lema del estado</u>
Esto perpetua
"Es eterno"

<u>State Flower</u>
Syringa

<u>Flor del estado</u>
Jeringuilla

<u>State Bird</u>
Mountain bluebird

<u>Ave del estado</u>
Azulejo de la montaña

<u>State Nicknames</u>
The Gem State and Gem
of the Mountains

<u>Motes del estado</u>
El Estado Gema y la
Gema de las Montañas

<u>State Tree</u>
Western White Pine

<u>Árbol del estado</u>
Pino blanco americano

<u>State Song</u>
"Here We Have Idaho"

<u>Canción del estado</u>
"Aquí está Idaho"

<u>State Gemstone</u>
Star garnet

<u>Piedra preciosa</u>
Granate estrellado

# Famous Idahoans/Idahoanos famosos

**Sacagawea**
*(1786?–1812)*

Indian guide
Guía indígena

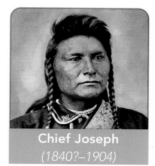

**Chief Joseph**
*(1840?–1904)*

Native American leader
Líder nativoamericano

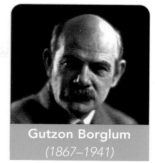

**Gutzon Borglum**
*(1867–1941)*

Sculptor
Escultor

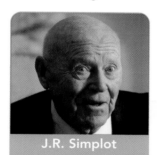

**J.R. Simplot**
*(1909–    )*

Industrialist
Industrial

**Frank Church**
*(1924–1984)*

U.S. senator
Senador de E.U.A.

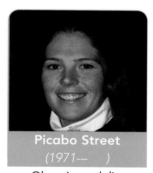

**Picabo Street**
*(1971—    )*

Olympic medalist
Campeona olímpica

# Words to Know/Palabras que debes saber

**border**
frontera

**explorers**
exploradores

**gemstone**
piedra
preciosa

**raft**
navegar en
balsa

# Here are more books to read about Idaho:
## Otros libros que puedes leer sobre Idaho:

**In English/En inglés:**

*Idaho: The Gem State*
World Almanac Library
of the States
by Edwards, Karen
World Almanac Library, 2003

*Idaho*
America the Beautiful
by George, Charles and
George, Linda
Children's Press, 2000

Words in English: 293

Palabras en español: 334

# Index

# Índice